KU-433-440

2 2 JUL 2024

WITHDRAWN

# FIRST SPANISH

# los animales, mis amigos

Consultant: Jeanine Beck

LORENZ BOOKS

# Contents

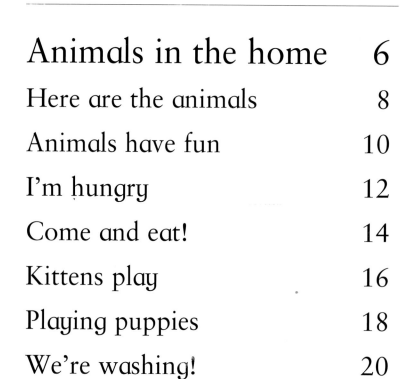

Leabharlann
Chontae Uíbh Fhailí
Class:
Acc:
Inv:

# Learning Spanish

Introduce your child to Spanish from an early age by combining everyday words and phrases with lively photographs of animals big and small, on the farm, in the wild and around the home. Your child will enjoy learning Spanish. Let them look at the pictures and read and remember the Spanish words and phrases that accompany them. Say the words aloud.

 ## A NEW LANGUAGE

There is a growing need today for everyone to speak a second language. All children should have the chance early in life to have access to a new language. Research indicates that children aged 2–8 are most receptive to linguistic learning. The younger the child, the easier it is to learn. The Spanish used in Europe differs from that spoken in Latin America and the United States in pronunciation and some vocabulary. The most noticeable difference in European Spanish pronunciation is the 'th' sound as in 'cena' (theh-na) or 'zapato' (tha-pat-oh). This is pronounced in America as 's' – 'seh-na', 'sa-pat-oh'.

## PRACTISING TOGETHER

Children love animals, so this theme is a perfect one for introducing them to Spanish. Encourage them to look at animals, birds and other creatures and say the Spanish words aloud. They can use their new Spanish vocabulary around the home with their pets, whenever they go out for a walk and at the zoo or nature reserve. You may have some Spanish friends who can talk to your children. All this will give your children a brilliant head start when they begin formal Spanish lessons at school.

## LEARNING WITH PICTURES

Children respond very well to photographs and will enjoy finding pictures of their favourite animals in this book. Help them say and learn the Spanish words for all sorts of pets, from cats and dogs to rabbits and guinea pigs. They'll discover the names of many wild animals and farm animals, too, from giraffes, leopards and elephants to ducklings, sheep and pigs. Let them use Spanish to count the animals or tell you what colours they are.

## IT'S FUN TO LEARN

Make learning fun by using the vocabulary on an everyday basis. Children like to demonstrate what they have learnt by playing games. You could mime an animal or imitate the noise an animal makes and ask your child to say its name in Spanish. Children can build up in a fun way their knowledge of commonly used Spanish words and phrases. This will give them the confidence to speak Spanish.

uno

dos

tres

cuatro

## HOW THE BOOK IS STRUCTURED

The key words on each page are highlighted and translated in vocabulary panels. Sentences on each page appear in both Spanish and English to help your child understand. At the end of every section is a question-and-answer game with a puzzle for you to do together and give the child a real sense of achievement. There is a special section on grammar, with a guide to pronunciation. The dictionary lists all the key words and explains how they should be pronounced. Reward certificates at the end of the book encourage your child to test their knowledge of Spanish and will also help develop their confidence and self-esteem.

# Los animales en casa

Animals in the home are friendly.
Pets like to live with people.
Talk to playful puppies, naughty
little kittens and grown-up cats.
They'll understand you when
you speak Spanish!

# Aquí están los animales

Here are the animals and birds. They have heads and eyes and legs, just like us.

¡Hola! Soy Isabel.
Hello! I am Isabel.

la niña

Y yo soy Milena.
And I am Milena.

la cola

la cabeza

Isabel

Milena

el gato

los ojos

la pata

| | la niña | el niño | la cabeza | los ojos |
|---|---|---|---|---|
| Say it with me | girl | boy | head | eyes |

# ¿Qué haces, Joel?
## What are you doing, Joel?

el pájaro

Joel

## Vuelo como un pájaro.
### I am flying like a bird.

el perro

el niño

## Y yo salto.
### And I am jumping.

| la pata | la cola | el gato | el perro | el pájaro |
|---------|---------|---------|----------|-----------|
| paw | tail | cat | dog | bird |

# Los animales se divierten

Animals have fun. They swim and jump just like us. But we can't fly – or make honey!

**¡Mira las abejas!**
Look at the bees!

la antena

cinco abejas

el ala

**Elaboran miel.**
They make honey.

la miel

Say it with me

| la antena | el ala | cinco abejas | la miel |
|-----------|--------|--------------|---------|
| antenna | wing | five bees | honey |

# Salto como una rana.
## I'm hopping like a frog.

cuatro ranas

la pata

la mano

# Sabemos nadar como peces.
## We can swim like fish.

la aleta

el pez de colores

|  |  |  |  |  |
|---|---|---|---|---|
| cuatro ranas | la pata | la mano | el pez de colores | la aleta |
| *four frogs* | *leg* | *hand* | *goldfish* | *fin* |

# Tengo hambre

I'm hungry. The animals are hungry. Come and help the animals choose their favourite foods.

Simón

¿Tienes hambre?
Are you hungry?

Sí, Simón, tengo hambre.
Yes, Simon, I am hungry.

el perro

la carne

Say it with me

| el perro | la carne | las galletas |
| dog | meat | biscuits |

12

# ¿Qué quieres comer?
## What would you like to eat?

¿unas galletas?

¿unas zanahorias?

el conejo

¿unas cebollas?

¿queso?

# ¡Me gustan las zanahorias!
## I like carrots!

| las zanahorias | el queso | las cebollas | el conejo |
|---|---|---|---|
| carrots | cheese | onions | rabbit |

13

# ¡A la mesa!

Come and eat! Some animals like to be fed. Other animals catch their own dinner when they can.

## ¿Quieres una manzana?
Would you like an apple?

Manuel

el conejo

la lechuga

## Sí, por favor, Manuel.
Yes, please, Manuel.

la cobaya

Say it with me

la manzana
apple

la lechuga
lettuce

el conejo
rabbit

la cobaya
guinea pig

# ¿Qué te gusta comer?
## What do you like to eat?

¿leche?

el gatito

¿dos ratones?

¿tres peces?

¿un helado?

## Nos gustan los peces.
### We like fish.

| **el gatito** | **la leche** | **el helado** | **dos ratones** | **tres peces** |
|:---:|:---:|:---:|:---:|:---:|
| kitten | milk | ice cream | two mice | three fish |

# Los gatitos juegan

Kittens play. They like chasing wool, running after balls and jumping as high as they can.

¡Mira el pequeño gatito!
Look at the little kitten!

Me gusta jugar.
I like to play.

la silla

el gatito malo

Say it with me

| la silla | el gatito malo | los juguetes | el gatito castaño |
|---|---|---|---|
| chair | naughty kitten | toys | ginger kitten |

los juguetes

## ¡Atrapa al ratón!
### Catch the mouse!

el gatito castaño

el gatito peludo

el gatito que salta

## Jugamos juntos.
### We are playing together.

el gatito rápido

el gatito lento

la pelota

|  |  |  |  |  |
|---|---|---|---|---|
| el gatito peludo | el gatito que salta | el gatito lento | la pelota | el gatito rápido |
| *fluffy kitten* | *jumping kitten* | *slow kitten* | *ball* | *fast kitten* |

# Los cachorros juegan

Playing puppies have lots of energy. They love to run and play all day until it's time for bed.

Paseo a mi cachorro por el parque.
I am taking my puppy to the park.

¿Te puedo acompañar?
Can I come too?

la correa verde

las patas

el hueso de goma

Say it with me

| la correa verde | el hueso de goma | las patas |
|---|---|---|
| green lead | rubber bone | paws |

18

# Jugamos con cuatro pelotas.
## We are playing with four balls.

uno

dos

el cachorro

tres

cuatro

# Tengo una pelota azul muy grande.
## I have a big blue ball.

# El cachorro está cansado.
## The puppy is tired.

una pelota azul muy grande

el cachorro dormido

tres pelotas azules
three blue balls

el cachorro
puppy

la pelota azul muy grande
big blue ball

el cachorro dormido
sleepy puppy

# ¡Nos bañamos!

We're washing! Cats can spend hours washing themselves, and dogs like having their fur brushed.

Me lavo.

I am washing.

el champú

el jabón

la bañera

la esponja

la toalla

los patitos de goma

Me gustan las burbujas de jabón.

I like soap bubbles.

| | | | | |
|---|---|---|---|---|
| Say it with me | la bañera<br>bath | el jabón<br>soap | la toalla<br>towel | el champú<br>shampoo |

# Estamos muy limpios.
We're very clean.

dos perros

## Me cepillo el pelo.
I am brushing my hair.

el cepillo para el pelo

## ¿Me quieres cepillar?
Will you brush me?

**el patito de goma**
rubber duck

**la esponja**
sponge

**dos perros**
two dogs

**el cepillo para el pelo**
hairbrush

# Es hora de ir a la cama

It's bedtime and everyone is tired. Let's get ready for bed and make sure the animals are comfy.

**Buenas noches a todos.**
Good night, everyone.

la cesta

el gato atigrado

**Estamos muy cansados.**
We are very tired.

el gato rayado

Say it with me

el osito
teddy bear

la cesta
basket

el gato atigrado
tabby cat

22

# Siempre tengo sueño.
## I'm always sleepy.

Lulú

la tortuga

Felipe y Frida

# ¿Quién duerme en la cesta?
## Who is sleeping in the basket?

el sueño

el perro marrón

# Estoy soñando.
## I am dreaming.

| | | | |
|---|---|---|---|
|  |  |  |  |
| **el gato rayado** | **la tortuga** | **el perro marrón** | **el sueño** |
| striped cat | tortoise | brown dog | dream |

# Puzzle time

Here are the animals you met, but can you remember their names? Here are some clues to help you. All their names are in the word square.

El cachorro camina.

The _ _ _ _ _ _ is walking.

Los peces nadan.

The _ _ _ _ are swimming.

El conejo come.

The _ _ _ _ _ _ _ is eating.

Las abejas zumban.

The _ _ _ _ are buzzing.

El gatito juega.

The _ _ _ _ _ _ is playing.

El perro salta.

The _ _ _ jumps.

Find all the Spanish words in my word square

¿Dónde está el gato?

Where is the _ _ _ ?

| p | e | r | r | o | v | x | c |
| e | w | b | h | o | c | e | a |
| c | a | b | e | j | a | s | c |
| e | l | o | f | a | r | k | h |
| s | e | g | a | t | i | t | o |
| t | k | o | e | p | r | u | r |
| g | a | t | o | t | n | o | r |
| z | s | c | o | n | e | j | o |

# Busca
# los animales

Look for the animals. You can find them in the home, in the garden and down on the farm. Look at the pictures and then say the words aloud. You're speaking Spanish!

# ¿Dónde viven?

Where do they live? Each animal has a favourite place to live. They feel safe inside their homes.

**El cachorro vive en una caseta.**
The puppy lives in a kennel.

la caseta

**Al cachorro le gusta su caseta.**
The puppy likes his kennel.

Say it with me

la caseta del perro
kennel

la jaula
cage

el gato tricolor
tortoiseshell cat

# ¿Qué casa para qué animal?
## Which house for which animal?

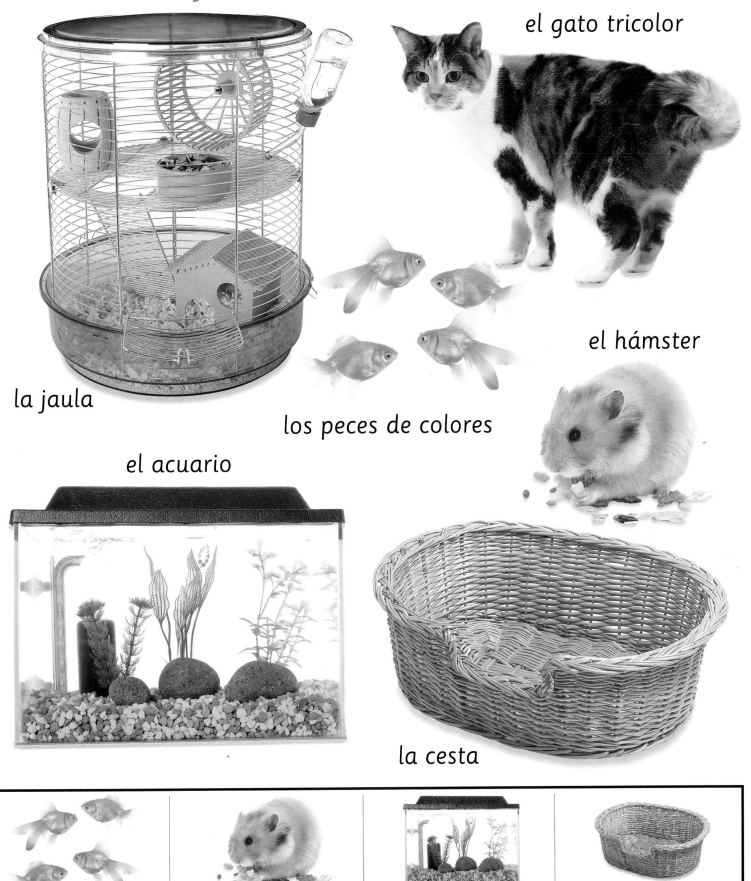

el gato tricolor

la jaula

los peces de colores

el acuario

el hámster

la cesta

| los peces de colores | el hámster | el acuario | la cesta |
| --- | --- | --- | --- |
| goldfish | hamster | aquarium | basket |

# La casa de mis sueños

My dream home is beautiful! All these animals live in beautiful homes. Which one would you like?

### ¿Dónde vives?
Where do you live?

la cuerda

el barco

### Vivo en un barco.
I live on a boat.

Say it with me

el barco
boat

la cuerda
rope

el castillo grande
big castle

# Vivimos en una casa pequeña.
We live in a little house.

el castillo grande

la casa pequeña

la puerta

# Vivo en un castillo grande.
I live in a big castle.

el piso

# Vivimos en un piso.
We live in a flat.

la ventana

|  |  |  |  |
|---|---|---|---|
| la casa pequeña | el piso | la puerta | la ventana |
| little house | flat | door | window |

# Los animales del jardín

Garden creatures come in all sizes and colours!
Some get food from the plants in the garden.

¿Cuántas mariposas hay?

*How many butterflies are there?*

las mariposas

la planta

el gato

la mariposa azul

Clara

¡Hay cuatro mariposas, Clara!

*There are four butterflies, Clara!*

Say it with me

la planta
plant

la mariposa azul
blue butterfly

el gato
cat

el caracol
snail

# ¿Cuántos bichos hay en cada grupo?
How many creatures are in each group?

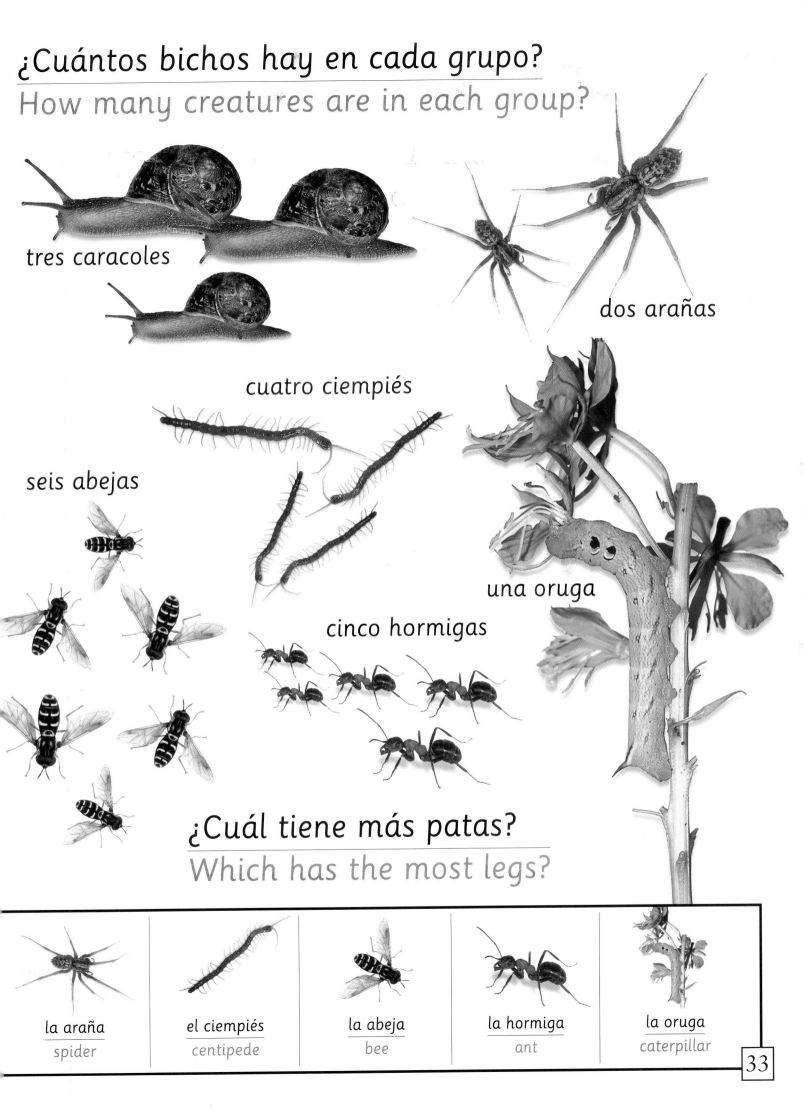

tres caracoles

dos arañas

cuatro ciempiés

seis abejas

una oruga

cinco hormigas

## ¿Cuál tiene más patas?
Which has the most legs?

la araña
spider

el ciempiés
centipede

la abeja
bee

la hormiga
ant

la oruga
caterpillar

# Mis amigos del jardín

Garden friends can be friendly or shy. You can put out food and water for the animals and birds.

**Estamos en el jardín.**
We are in the garden.

las macetas

**Planta la lechuga, por favor.**
Please plant some lettuce.

el conejo

la cobaya

Say it with me

| | | | | |
|---|---|---|---|---|
| el conejo<br>rabbit | la cobaya<br>guinea pig | las macetas<br>flowerpots | la ardilla<br>squirrel |

la ardilla

¿Cuántos animales hay?
How many animals are there?

las mariquitas

Hay doce animales.
There are twelve animals.

el pájaro l'oiseau

la tortuga

dos ranas

| el pájaro | la regadera | la tortuga | las mariquitas | la rana |
|-----------|-------------|------------|----------------|---------|
| bird | watering can | tortoise | ladybirds | frog |

35

# En la granja

On the farm, it's fun to look after the animals.
There are lots of different animals and birds.

¿Has perdido a tu mamá?

Have you lost your mummy?

el ternero

Sí, he perdido a mi mamá.

Yes, I have lost my mummy.

Say it with me

| el ternero | el cerdo | la vaca |
|------------|----------|---------|
| calf | pig | cow |

# ¿Puedes ayudar a estas madres a encontrar a sus bebés?

## Can you help these mothers find their babies?

los patitos

la vaca

el cerdo

los pollitos

el cerdito

el pato

la gallina

| el patito | el pollito | el pato | el cerdito | la gallina |
|-----------|------------|---------|------------|------------|
| duckling | chick | duck | piglet | hen |

# Los animales en la granja

Farm animals need to be cared for and fed. The sheepdog helps the farmer look after the sheep.

¿Qué haces?

What are you doing?

el perro pastor

el tractor

Busco los corderos.

I am looking for the sheep.

Say it with me

el tractor
tractor

el perro pastor
sheepdog

la granja
farm

# Diana da de comer a sus animales.
## Diana is feeding her animals.

Diana

la granja

## ¿Qué comen estos animales?
### What do these animals eat?

¿manzanas?

el cordero

el caballo

¿hierba?

¿heno?

| | | | | |
|---|---|---|---|---|
| la manzana | el cordero | la hierba | el caballo | el heno |
| apple | sheep | grass | horse | hay |

39

# Puzzle time

Animals come in all shapes and sizes, but who is the biggest and who is the smallest? Complete the Lost Letters puzzle with their names.

¿Es un hámster más grande que una vaca?

Is a _____ bigger than a ____?

Las hormigas son muy pequeñas.

The ____ are very small.

¿Es Carlos más pequeño que un patito?

Is Carlos smaller than a _____?.

¿Es un caballo más grande que un gato?

Is a _ _ _ _ _ _ bigger than a _ _ _ ?

Find the lost Spanish letters

El conejo es pequeño.

The _ _ _ _ _ _ _ is small.

El cerdo está muy gordo.

The _ _ _ is very fat.

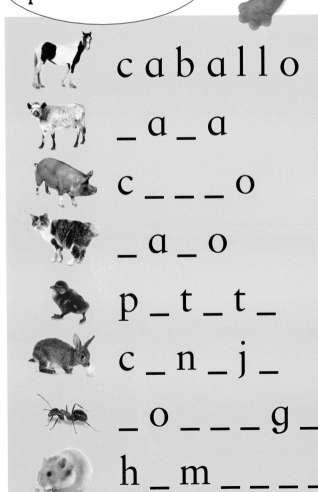

c a b a l l o

_ a _ a

c _ _ _ o

_ a _ o

p _ t _ t _

c _ n _ j _

_ o _ _ _ g _

h _ m _ _ _ _

41

# Recorrer el mundo

Around the world are many exciting animals. You can read about them now, and one day you may see them all. Get ready by learning their Spanish names and saying the words aloud.

# El bosque

The forest is a wonderful place to walk. You can find all sorts of wild animals.

Paula

Paula juega en el bosque.
Paula is playing in the forest.

las avellanas

la piña de pino

las hojas

la hiedra

¿Qué ha encontrado?
What has she found?

Say it with me

las hojas
leaves

la piña de pino
pine cone

las avellanas
hazelnuts

las cochinillas
woodlice

# ¿Cuántos animales ves?

## How many animals can you see?

el águila

el búho

el conejo tímido

las cochinillas

el zorro

el águila
eagle

el búho
owl

el conejo tímido
timid rabbit

la hiedra
ivy

el zorro
fox

45

# En la costa

On the seashore you can find all kinds of animals.
Look for them in rock pools and by the sea.

Isabel

¿Qué busca Isabel?

What is Isabel looking for?

las conchas

la estrella de mar

el frailecillo

la arena

Say it with me

la concha
shell

la arena
sand

la estrella de mar
starfish

el frailecillo
puffin

# ¿Quién nada en el agua?
## Who is swimming in the water?

las gaviotas

el sol

los peces

el delfín

el cangrejo

**la gaviota**
seagull

**el sol**
sun

**el pez**
fish

**el cangrejo**
crab

**el delfín**
dolphin

# La pradera

The grasslands are an exciting place to watch wild animals. But be careful not to get too close!

Pablo

los prismáticos

**Buenos días. ¿Cómo estás?**
Hello. How are you?

la jirafa

**Muy bien, Pablo. ¡Gracias!**
Very well, Pablo. Thank you!

Say it with me

los prismáticos
binoculars

la jirafa
giraffe

la cebra
zebra

# ¿Quién tiene la nariz más larga?
## Who has the longest nose?

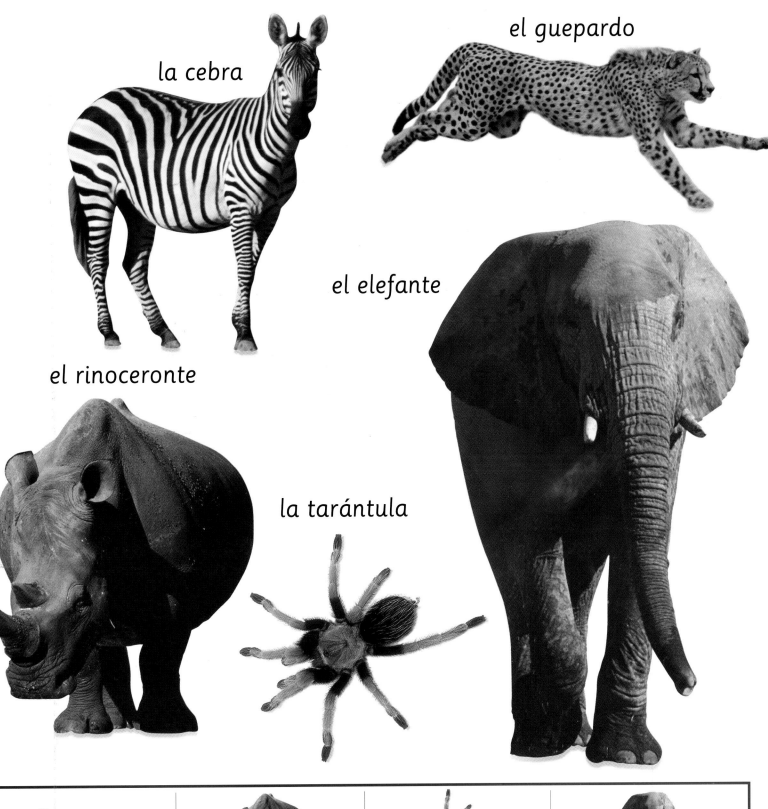

la cebra

el guepardo

el elefante

el rinoceronte

la tarántula

el guepardo
cheetah

el rinoceronte
rhinoceros

la tarántula
tarantula

el elefante
elephant

# En la nieve

In the snow, you'll find lots of animals that love the cold. Remember to wrap up warm!

el gorro

la bufanda

### Tengo bolas de nieve para jugar.
I have some snowballs.

### ¡No nos las tires!
Don't throw them at us!

los pingüinos

las botas

Say it with me

__el gorro__
hat

__la bufanda__
scarf

__la bola de nieve__
snowball

__la bota__
boot

# ¡Cuidado!
Look out!

la foca

los niños

# ¡Nos escondemos en la nieve!
We are hiding in the snow!

la búho
de las nieves

el oso polar

**el pingüino**
*penguin*

**la foca**
*seal*

**los niños**
*children*

**la búho de las nieves**
*snowy owl*

**el oso polar**
*polar bear*

# Las montañas

The mountains can be wild and dangerous.
Look out for eagles and wolves.

Antonio

## ¡Mira el halcón!
Look at the hawk!

el impermeable

el halcón

## ¡No me atrapará, Antonio!
He won't catch me, Antonio!

el leopardo

| | | | | |
|---|---|---|---|---|
| Say it with me | el impermeable<br>raincoat | <br>el halcón<br>hawk | el leopardo<br>leopard | <br>el buitre<br>vulture |

# Volamos.
## We are flying.

el ala

el buitre

el águila

# Puedo escalar.
## I can climb.

los cuernos

# ¡Soy muy feroz!
## I am very fierce!

la cabra

el lobo

|  |  |  |  |  |
|---|---|---|---|---|
| **el ala**<br>wing | **el águila**<br>eagle | **la cabra**<br>goat | **el cuerno**<br>horn | **el lobo**<br>wolf |

# La jungla

The jungle is home to many brightly coloured animals. But you can't see them when they hide!

¡Soy un tigre!
I am a tiger!

¡Qué loro más bonito!
What a beautiful parrot!

la pluma

el loro

la pluma
feather

el loro
parrot

el pelaje
fur

Say it with me

# ¿Quién es distinto?

Who is the odd one out?

el tigre

el pelaje

la serpiente

# ¡Soy yo! ¡No tengo rayas!

It's me! I don't have stripes!

la rana

el camaleón

| el tigre | la serpiente | la rana | el camaleón |
|----------|--------------|---------|-------------|
| tiger | snake | frog | chameleon |

# Puzzle time

Pablo is trying to find animals of different colours. Can you help him fill in the sentences? Use the Spanish words to fill in the crossword.

**1 El elefante es gris.**
The elephant is _ _ _ _ _.

Pablo

**2 Las mariquitas son rojas.**
The ladybirds are _ _ _ _.

**3 El ala del loro es azul.**
The parrot's wing is _ _ _ _ _.

**4 El pecho del loro es amarillo.**
The parrot's chest is _ _ _ _ _ _ _.

**5 La tarántula es marrón.**
The tarantula is _ _ _ _ _ _.

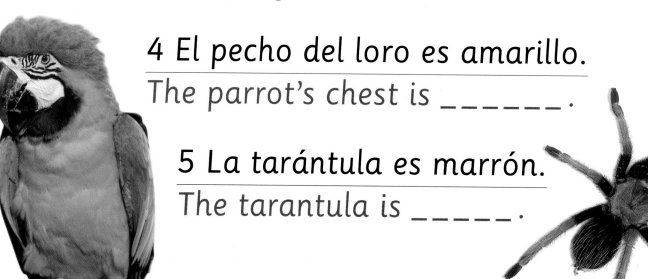

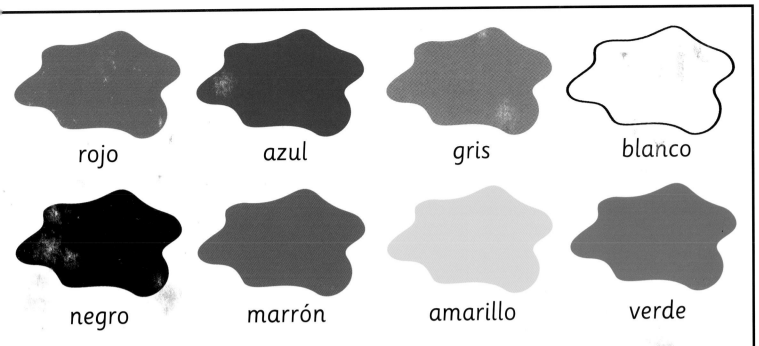

rojo

azul

gris

blanco

negro

marrón

amarillo

verde

**6 La cabeza del pingüino es negra.**

The penguin's head is _ _ _ _ _ _ .

**7 El pecho del pingüino es blanco.**

The penguin's chest is _ _ _ _ _ _ .

Now try my crossword!

**8 La rana es verde.**

The frog is _ _ _ _ _ _ .

# How Spanish works

Encourage your child to enjoy learning Spanish and go further in the language. You may find these basic tips on how the Spanish language works helpful. Check out the dictionary, since it lists all the key words in the book and will help you pronounce the words correctly to your child.

## MASCULINE/FEMININE

All nouns in Spanish are either masculine (el, un) or feminine (la, una), but this bears no relation to the actual gender of the animal (so a male tortoise is still 'la tortuga'). 'Los' or 'unos' are used in the plural for masculine nouns, 'las' or 'unas' for feminine nouns.

## ADJECTIVES

As a general rule, feminine adjectives end in 'a' (e.g. la niña pequeña) and masculine adjectives in 'o' (e.g. el niño pequeño). If the adjective does not end in 'o' or 'a' it does not change.

## COMPARING THINGS

When we want to compare things in English, we say they are, for example, small, smaller or smallest. This is the pattern in Spanish:

| SPANISH | ENGLISH |
| --- | --- |
| Es pequeño | He is small |
| Es más pequeño | He is smaller |
| Es el más pequeño | He is the smallest |

## PERSONAL PRONOUNS

Remember that 'él' is masculine and 'ella' is feminine. The plurals are 'ellos' and 'ellas'.

| SPANISH | ENGLISH |
| --- | --- |
| yo | I |
| tú | you (singular) |
| usted | you (singular polite) |
| él or ella | he or she |
| nosotros | we |
| vosotros | you (plural) |
| ustedes | you (plural polite) |
| ellos or ellas | they |

'Tú' and 'vosotros' (plural) are used for talking to people you know. 'Usted' and 'ustedes' (plural) are used when you are talking to someone you don't know and are being polite.

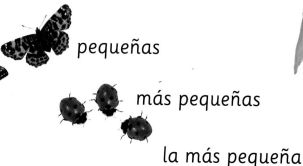

pequeñas

más pequeñas

la más pequeña

Es un niño.

Es una niña.

## VERBS

Spanish verbs change their endings depending on which personal pronoun and tense are used. This book uses only the present tense but there are other tenses in Spanish including the past and the future.

Help your child find the language pattern that emerges in the endings of the verbs. There are three groups of verbs which follow a regular pattern: those ending in 'ar', 'er' and 'ir'. Point out that in the verbs given here, 'tú' either ends in '-as' or '-es' and 'usted' either in '-a' or '-e' whilst 'vosotros' ends in '-áis', 'éis' or 'ís' and 'ustedes' in '-an' or '-en'. Play a game by saying the first word aloud – 'Yo', 'Tú'. Let your child answer with the verb – 'salto', 'saltas'.

Here are three simple verbs in the present tense. Look at the ends of the words and say the Spanish out loud.

| SPANISH | ENGLISH |
| --- | --- |
| **saltar** | **to jump** |
| Yo salto | I jump |
| Tú saltas | You jump |
| Usted salta | You jump (polite) |
| Él/ella salta | He/she jumps |
| Nosotros saltamos | We jump |
| Vosotros saltáis | You jump |
| Ustedes saltan | You jump (plural polite) |
| Ellos/ellas saltan | They jump |

| SPANISH | ENGLISH |
| --- | --- |
| **comer** | **to eat** |
| Yo como | I eat |
| Tú comes | You eat |
| Usted come | You eat (polite) |
| Él/ella come | He/she eats |
| Nosotros comemos | We eat |
| Vosotros coméis | You eat |
| Ustedes comen | You eat (plural polite) |
| Ellos/ellas comen | They eat |

| SPANISH | ENGLISH |
| --- | --- |
| **decir** | **to say** |
| Yo digo | I say |
| Tú dices | You say |
| Usted dice | You say (polite) |
| Él/ella dice | He/she says |
| Nosotros decimos | We say |
| Vosotros decís | You say |
| Ustedes dicen | You say (pl. polite) |
| Ellos/ellas dicen | They say |

# Pronunciation Key

| SPANISH | PRONOUNCE | EXAMPLE |
| --- | --- | --- |
| a | a | pato: pa-toh |
| ai | eye | frailecillo: fry-leh-thee-yo |
| e | eh | carne: kar-neh |
| u | oo | tortuga: tor-too-ga |
| ui | wee | buitre: bwee-treh |
| b | b | barco: bar-koh |
| v | b | gaviota: ga-bee-ota |
| c | k | casa: ka-sa |
| c | th | cepillo: theh-pee-yoh |
| h | this is not pronounced | hormiga: or-mee-ga |
| g | h | gemelos: hem-el-oz |
| j | h | jaula: how-la |
| gu | g | águila: a-gi-la |
| ll | y | gallina: ga-yee-na |
| ñ | ny | niña: nee-nya |
| qu | k | pequeño: pe-ke-nyo |
| z | th | zanahoria: thana-or-ee-a |

# El diccionario

| ENGLISH | SPANISH | SAY |
|---|---|---|

## A

| ant | la hormiga | *la or-mee-ga* |
| antenna | la antena | *la an-ten-a* |
| apple | la manzana | *la man-than-a* |
| aquarium | el acuario | *el ak-war-ee-oh* |

## B

| ball | la pelota | *la pel-oh-ta* |
| balls | las pelotas | *las pel-oh-taz* |
| basket | la cesta | *la thes-ta* |
| bath | la bañera | *la ban-yehr-a* |
| bed | la cama | *la ka-ma* |
| bee | la abeja | *la ab-eh-ha* |
| bees | las abejas | *las ab-eh-haz* |
| big | grande | *gran-deh* |
| binoculars | los prismáticos | *los priz-mat-ikoz* |
| bird | el pájaro | *el pa-ha-roh* |
| birds | los pájaros | *los pa-ha-roz* |
| biscuits | las galletas | *las ga-yet-az* |
| boat | el barco | *el bar-koh* |
| boot | la bota | *la boh-ta* |
| boy | el niño | *el nee-nyo* |
| boys | los niños | *los nee-nyoz* |
| butterfly | la mariposa | *la mar-ee-poh-sa* |

## Colours

| ENGLISH | SPANISH | SAY |
|---|---|---|
| black | negro | *neh-groh* |
| blue | azul | *a-thool* |
| brown | marrón | *mar-ron* |
| green | verde | *behr-deh* |
| grey | gris | *grees* |
| pink | rosa | *roh-sa* |
| red | rojo | *roh-hoh* |
| white | blanco | *blan-koh* |
| yellow | amarillo | *am-ar-ee-yoh* |

## Days of the week

| ENGLISH | SPANISH | SAY |
|---|---|---|
| Monday | lunes | *loo-nez* |
| Tuesday | martes | *mar-tez* |
| Wednesday | miércoles | *mee-ehr-koh-lez* |
| Thursday | jueves | *hweh-bez* |
| Friday | viernes | *bee-ehr-nez* |
| Saturday | sábado | *sa-ba-doh* |
| Sunday | domingo | *do-ming-goh* |

| ENGLISH | SPANISH | SAY |
|---|---|---|

## C

| cage | la jaula | *la how-la* |
| calf | el ternero | *el tehr-neh-roh* |
| carrots | las zanahorias | *las thana-or-ee-az* |
| castle | el castillo | *el kas-tee-yoh* |
| cat | el gato | *el ga-toh* |
| caterpillar | la oruga | *la or-oo-ga* |
| centipede | el ciempiés | *el thee-em-pee-ez* |
| chair | la silla | *la see-ya* |
| chameleon | el camaleón | *el ka-mal-eh-on* |
| cheese | el queso | *el keh-soh* |
| cheetah | el guepardo | *el gay-par-doh* |
| chick | el pollito | *el poh-yee-toh* |
| children | los niños | *los nee-nyoz* |
| coat | el abrigo | *el ab-ree-goh* |
| cow | la vaca | *la ba-ka* |
| crab | el cangrejo | *el kan-greh-hoh* |

## D

| dirty | sucio | *soo-thee-oh* |
| dog | el perro | *el per-roh* |
| dolphin | el delfín | *el del-feen* |
| door | la puerta | *la pwehr-ta* |
| dream | el sueño | *el sweh-nyoh* |
| duck | el pato | *el pa-toh* |
| duckling | el patito | *el pa-tee-toh* |

# E

| English | Spanish | Say |
|---------|---------|-----|
| eagle | el águila | *el a-gi-la* |
| ear | la oreja | *la or-eh-ha* |
| elephant | el elefante | *el eleh-fan-teh* |
| eyes | los ojos | *los oh-hoz* |

# F

| English | Spanish | Say |
|---------|---------|-----|
| fast | rápido | *ra-pi-doh* |
| feather | la pluma | *la ploo-ma* |
| fin | la aleta | *la al-eh-ta* |
| fish | el pez | *el peth* |
| fishes | los peces | *los pe-thez* |
| flat | el piso | *el pee-soh* |
| flowerpot | la maceta | *la ma-theh-ta* |
| fluffy | peludo | *peh-loo-doh* |
| fox | el zorro | *el thor-roh* |
| frog | la rana | *la ra-na* |
| frogs | las ranas | *las ra-naz* |
| fur | el pelaje | *el pel-a-heh* |

# G

| English | Spanish | Say |
|---------|---------|-----|
| ginger | castaño | *ka-sta-nyoh* |
| giraffe | la jirafa | *la hee-raf-a* |
| girl | la niña | *la nee-nya* |
| girls | las niñas | *las nee-nyaz* |
| goat | la cabra | *la ka-bra* |
| goldfish | los peces de colores | *los pe-thez deh ko-lor-ez* |
| grass | la hierba | *la yehr-ba* |
| guinea pig | la cobaya | *la ko-ba-ya* |

# H

| English | Spanish | Say |
|---------|---------|-----|
| hairbrush | el cepillo para el pelo | *el theh-pee-yoh para el peh-loh* |
| hamster | el hámster | *el ham-stehr* |
| hand | la mano | *la ma-noh* |
| hat | el gorro | *el gor-roh* |
| hawk | el halcón | *el al-kon* |
| hay | el heno | *el eh-noh* |
| hazelnuts | las avellanas | *las abeh-yan-az* |
| head | la cabeza | *la ka-beh-tha* |
| hen | la gallina | *la ga-yee-na* |
| honey | la miel | *la mee-yel* |
| horn | el cuerno | *el kwehr-noh* |
| horse | el caballo | *el ka-ba-yoh* |
| house | la casa | *la ka-sa* |

# I

| English | Spanish | Say |
|---------|---------|-----|
| ice cream | el helado | *el eh-la-doh* |
| ivy | la hiedra | *la yeh-dra* |

# K

| English | Spanish | Say |
|---------|---------|-----|
| kennel | la caseta del perro | *la ka-seh-ta del per-roh* |
| kitten | el gatito | *el ga-tee-toh* |

# L

| English | Spanish | Say |
|---------|---------|-----|
| ladybirds | las mariquitas | *las ma-ree-kee-taz* |
| lead | la correa | *la kor-reh-a* |
| leaves | las hojas | *las oh-haz* |
| leg | la pata | *la pa-ta* |
| leopard | el guepardo | *el gay-par-doh* |
| lettuce | la lechuga | *la leh-choo-ga* |
| little | pequeño | *pe-ke-nyo* |

# M

| English | Spanish | Say |
|---------|---------|-----|
| meat | la carne | *la kar-neh* |
| mice | los ratones | *los ra-toh-nez* |
| milk | la leche | *la leh-cheh* |
| mouse | el ratón | *el ra-ton* |

# Months of the year

| ENGLISH | SPANISH | SAY |
|---------|---------|-----|
| January | enero | *en-ehr-oh* |
| February | febrero | *feb-rehr-oh* |
| March | marzo | *mar-thoh* |
| April | abril | *ab-reel* |
| May | mayo | *ma-yoh* |
| June | junio | *hoo-nee-oh* |
| July | julio | *hoo-lee-oh* |
| August | agosto | *ag-ost-oh* |
| September | septiembre | *sep-tee-em-breh* |
| October | octubre | *ok-too-breh* |
| November | noviembre | *nob-ee-em-breh* |
| December | diciembre | *dith-ee-em-breh* |

| ENGLISH | SPANISH | SAY |
|---|---|---|

## N and O

| | | |
|---|---|---|
| naughty | malo | *ma-loh* |
| onions | las cebollas | *las theh-boy-az* |
| owl | el búho | *el boo-oh* |

## P

| | | |
|---|---|---|
| parrot | el loro | *el lo-roh* |
| paw | la pata | *la pa-ta* |
| penguin | el pingüino | *el pin-gwee-noh* |
| pig | el cerdo | *el thehr-doh* |
| piglet | el cerdito | *el thehr-dee-toh* |
| pine cone | la piña de pino | *la pee-nya deh pee-noh* |
| plant | la planta | *la plan-ta* |
| polar bear | el oso polar | *el oh-soh poh-lar* |
| puffin | el frailecillo | *el fry-leh-thee-yoh* |
| puppy | el cachorro | *el ca-chor-roh* |

## R

| | | |
|---|---|---|
| rabbit | el conejo | *el kon-eh-hoh* |
| raincoat | el impermeable | *el im-pehr-meh-a-bleh* |
| rhinoceros | el rinoceronte | *el ree-noth-ehr-on-teh* |
| rope | la cuerda | *la kwehr-da* |
| rubber bone | el hueso de goma | *el weh-soh deh goh-ma* |
| rubber duck | el patito de goma | *el pa-tee-toh deh goh-ma* |

# Numbers

| | ENGLISH | SPANISH | SAY |
|---|---|---|---|
| 1 | one | uno (m.)/una (f.) | *oo-no/oo-na* |
| 2 | two | dos | *dos* |
| 3 | three | tres | *tres* |
| 4 | four | cuatro | *kwa-troh* |
| 5 | five | cinco | *thing-koh* |
| 6 | six | seis | *seh-ees* |
| 7 | seven | siete | *see-eh-teh* |
| 8 | eight | ocho | *och-oh* |
| 9 | nine | nueve | *noo-eh-beh* |
| 10 | ten | diez | *dee-eth* |

| ENGLISH | SPANISH | SAY |
|---|---|---|

## S

| | | |
|---|---|---|
| sand | la arena | *la ar-eh-na* |
| scarf | la bufanda | *la boo-fan-da* |
| seagull | la gaviota | *la ga-bee-oh-ta* |
| seal | la foca | *la foh-ka* |
| shampoo | el champú | *el cham-poo* |
| sheep | el cordero | *el kor-dehr-oh* |
| sheepdog | el perro pastor | *el per-roh pa-stor* |
| shell | la concha | *la kon-cha* |
| sleepy | dormido | *dor-mee-doh* |
| slow | lento | *len-toh* |
| small | pequeño | *pe-ke-nyoh* |
| snail | el caracol | *el kara-kol* |
| snake | la serpiente | *la sehr-pee-enteh* |
| snowball | la bola de nieve | *la boh-la deh nee-eh-beh* |
| snowy owl | el búho de las nieves | *el boo-oh deh las nee-eh-behz* |
| soap | el jabón | *el ha-bon* |
| spider | la araña | *la ar-anya* |
| sponge | la esponja | *la es-pong-ha* |
| spotty | manchado | *man-cha-doh* |
| squirrel | la ardilla | *la ar-dee-ya* |
| starfish | la estrella de mar | *la es-treh-ya deh mar* |
| striped | rayado | *ra-ya-doh* |
| sun | el sol | *el sol* |

## T and V

| | | |
|---|---|---|
| tail | la cola | *la koh-la* |
| tarantula | la tarántula | *la ta-ran-too-la* |
| teddy bear | el osito | *el os-ee-toh* |
| tiger | el tigre | *el tee-greh* |
| timid | tímido | *teem-i-doh* |
| tortoise | la tortuga | *la tor-too-ga* |
| towel | la toalla | *la toh-a-ya* |
| toys | los juguetes | *los hoo-geht-ehz* |
| tractor | el tractor | *el trak-tor* |
| vulture | el buitre | *el bwee-treh* |

## W and Z

| | | |
|---|---|---|
| watering can | la regadera | *la reh-ga-dehr-a* |
| window | la ventana | *la ben-ta-na* |
| wing | el ala | *el a-la* |
| wolf | el lobo | *el loh-boh* |
| woodlice | las cochinillas | *las koh-chee-nee-yaz* |
| zebra | la cebra | *la theh-bra* |

**This is to certify that**

_____

can count
from one to ten
in Spanish

Date _____

**This is to certify that**

_____

can say
six colours
in Spanish

Date _____

**This is to certify that**

_____

can say
six bird names
in Spanish

Date _____

**This is to certify that**

_____

can say
six animal names
in Spanish

Date _____

This edition is published by Lorenz Books

Lorenz Books is an imprint of Anness Publishing Ltd
Hermes House, 88–89 Blackfriars Road, London SE1 8HA
tel. 020 7401 2077; fax 020 7633 9499
www.lorenzbooks.com; info@anness.com

© Anness Publishing Ltd 2003

This edition distributed in the UK by The Manning Partnership Ltd, 6 The Old Dairy, Melcombe Road
Bath BA2 3LR; tel. 01225 478 444; fax 01225 478 440; sales@manning-partnership.co.uk

This edition distributed in the USA and Canada by National Book Network, 4720 Boston Way
Lanham, MD 20706; tel. 301 459 3366; fax 301 459 1705; www.nbnbooks.com

This edition distributed in Australia by Pan Macmillan Australia, Level 18, St Martins Tower
31 Market St, Sydney, NSW 2000; tel. 1300 135 113; fax 1300 135 103; customer.service@macmillan.com.au

This edition distributed in New Zealand by David Bateman Ltd, 30 Tarndale Grove, Off Bush Road
Albany, Auckland; tel. [09] 415 7664; fax [09] 415 8892

All rights reserved. No part of this publication may be reproduced, stored in a retrieval system, or transmitted
in any way or by any means, electronic, mechanical, photocopying, recording or otherwise, without the prior
written permission of the copyright holder.

A CIP catalogue record for this book is available from the British Library.

Publisher: Joanna Lorenz
Managing Editor: Linda Fraser
Editor: Joy Wotton
Editorial Consultant: Christine Younger
Design: Maggi Howells
Editorial Reader: Penelope Goodare
Photography: Jane Burton, John Daniels, John Freeman,
Robert Pickett, Kim Taylor, Lucy Tizard

The publishers would like to thank
all the children who appear in this book
and Martin B. Withers/FLPA – Images
of Nature for the photograph on
page 51 top right.

10 9 8 7 6 5 4 3 2 1

Y ahora,
¡tú sabes hablar
español!